# CHINA

**CHELSEA HOUSE**
PUBLISHERS
A Haights Cross Communications ⌐ Company ®
www.chelseahouse.com

First hardcover library edition published
in the United States of America in
2006 by Chelsea House Publishers,
a subsidiary of Haights Cross Communications.
All rights reserved.

A Haights Cross Communications  Company ®

www.chelseahouse.com

Library of Congress Cataloging-in-Publication
Gassos, Dolores.
  China / Dolores Gassos.
    p. cm.—(Ancient civilizations)
  Audience: Grades 4–6.
  ISBN 0-7910-8476-0
    1. China—Civilization—Juvenile literature.
I. Title. II. Ancient civilizations (Phalidelphia, Pa.).
DS721.G3183 2005
931-dc22
                2005006394

**Production and Realization**
Parramón Ediciones, S.A.

**Texts**
Dolores Gassós

**Translator**
Patrick Clark

**Graphic Design and Typesetting**
Estudi Toni Inglés (Alba Marco)

First edition: March 2005

Ancient Civilizations
China

Printed in Spain
© Parramón Ediciones, S.A. – 2005
Ronda de Sant Pere, 5, 4ª planta
08010 Barcelona (España)
Empresa del Grupo Editorial Norma

www.parramon.com

## TABLE OF CONTENTS

# A DISTANT AND FASCINATING EMPIRE

The history of a great civilization that lasted into the modern era began more than nine thousand years ago, in the immense territories of East Asia, irrigated by long and deep rivers that flow into the Pacific Ocean. In the year 7000 B.C., the first traces of the Chinese empires began to appear; they would collapse in 1911 after the overthrow of the last emperor. Under the rule of emperors, a meticulously structured society developed, and all the arts flourished.

The Chinese were brave warriors, but they also brought the arts of painting, literature, and philosophy to their greatest heights, while excellent craftsmen knew how to convert everyday objects into small works of art.

For all these reasons, we wish to awaken in young readers an interest in the passionate Chinese civilization with a brief historical introduction and a discussion of eleven topics that cover the most important aspects of this ancient and enduring civilization in words and pictures. The central image of each double page gives an immediate impression about the topic under discussion, while the text, which is informative and anecdotal at the same time, presents basic knowledge about the subject. At the end of the book, there is a chronology of the principal periods in Chinese history and a small list of interesting historical facts.

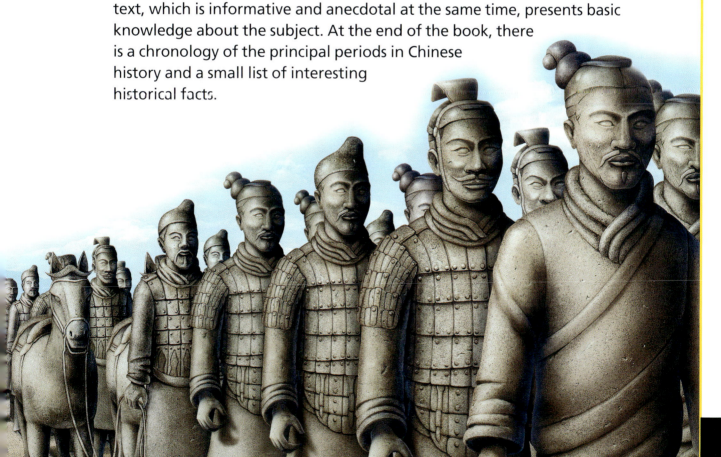

# CHINA'S TRADITION OF DYNASTIES

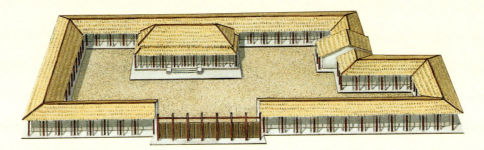

Reconstruction of an ancient Shang Palace, in Yashi (Henan providence), built more than thirty centuries ago.

## AN ANCIENT CIVILIZATION

China is a huge country and its physical geography is very complex. These circumstances help to explain some characteristics of this ancient civilization; for example, its isolation from other countries and cultures, the lack of drive to expand its already vast territory through military conquest, and the need to maintain cultural unity in the face of ethnic and geographic diversity.

Human beings lived in China as long as two million years ago, but the first stages of civilization go back to 7000 B.C. The Neolithic period, which lasted until 1500 B.C., brought with it the first settlements, based on agriculture and cattle raising.

The passage from prehistory to history in China occurs around the year 1500 B.C., when writing appeared; this period roughly coincides with the establishment of the Shang Dynasty, which governed the country from 1500 B.C. to 1050 B.C. The Shang Dynasty exercised control primarily in northern China, around the basin of the Huang He River. During the reign of the Shang Dynasty, techniques for making bronze were discovered, and a new social structure appeared, characterized by the concentration of power in the king. During this period, the population of China was between four or five million people. People lived mainly in towns, but some lived in walled cities that achieved a considerable level of development.

## FROM THE SEVEN KINGDOMS TO UNITY

Between the years 1050 B.C. and 221 B.C., the country was ruled by the Zhou Dynasty. The Zhou Dynasty is divided into two periods: the Western Zhou (1050–771 B.C.), with its capital in the area where present-day Xian is located, and the Eastern Zhou (771–221 B.C.), with its

Cross-section of a stove for melting copper, used in China more than twenty-five hundred years ago.

Figurine showing the horse and cart of a Han-era merchant (c. 100 B.C.).

capital in Luoyang. The Zhou Dynasty created a highly bureaucratic state. They were forced to move their capital to Luoyang, located further east, due to harassment by the nomadic people of western China. During their reign, iron metallurgy began. Using this new material, manufacture of farming tools, weapons, and ritual objects began.

The final stage of the Zhou Dynasty is subdivided into the "Era of Springs and Autumns" (722–481 B.C.) and the "Era of Fighting Kings" (481 B.C.–221 B.C.), during which China was divided into seven kingdoms, each of which took a chief role in a period of wars and constant confrontations. The most powerful and best-organized kingdoms were the Qin and the Wei. In the year 221 B.C., the ruler of the Qin kingdom defeated his enemies and succeeded in uniting China for the first time in its history. Thus arose the Qin Empire, governed by the first emperor, Qin Shi Huangdi, who established the capital in Xianyang. The construction of the Great Wall and

an imposing imperial mausoleum that broke with previous funerary traditions are also credited to Qin Shi Huangdi.

## THE HAN AND TANG DYNASTIES

The uprisings that followed the death of the first emperor ended the Qin Dynasty; it was succeeded by one of the most important lineages in the history of the country, the Han Dynasty (206 B.C.–220 A.D.), whose reign is divided into the West Han period (206 B.C–25 B.C.), with its capital city in Chang'an (today's Xian), and the East Han period (25 B.C.–220 A.D.), with the capital in Luoyang. During this era, the use of jade reached its peak. It was believed that jade could confer immortality; jade was therefore used to make burial shrouds and various funerary objects.

Han-period terracotta (206 B.C.–220 A.D.) representing a tomb in the shape of a watchtower.

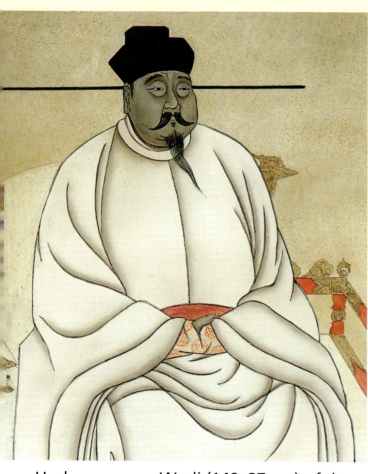

Emperor Taizu, founder of the Song Dynasty.

One of the twelve statues that line the sacred road leading to the tombs of the Ming emperors.

Under emperor Wudi (140–87 B.C.) of the Han Dynasty, general Zhan Qian carried out a series of expeditions to Central Asia. This was the beginning of the Silk Route. And it was the very merchants traveling along this commercial route, who introduced Buddhism to China. This philosophy of Hindu origin was quickly adopted by Chinese emperors as an official religion.

After the fall of the Han Dynasty, political unification was not achieved again until the installation of the Tang Dynasty (618–907). The pacification of a territory ruled by warring clans and dynasties was the work of Li Yuan, the first Tan emperor, who ruled under the name of Gaozu (618–626). The capital was established at Chang'an, which became a cosmopolitan center with a population exceeding two million people.

## THE SONG AND YUAN DYNASTIES

In the year 917, after the fall of the Tang Dynasty, a new period of struggles and political instability began. This period ended in the year 960 with a campaign of military annexation of the different kingdoms by the general Zhao Kuangyin. He founded the Northern Song Dynasty (1002–1127), ruling as emperor Taizu, and established his capital at Kaifeng, a great commercial and administrative city. Under the Song Dynasty, the art of making porcelain was discovered. For centuries, this would be one of China's most important artistic activities.

In the year 1127, the Mongols, a nomadic people from Central Asia, took Kaifeng, forcing the surviving members of the court to move to Hangzhou. The Southern Song Dynasty was established in this southern Chinese city. It endured until the Mongols ended it by capturing Hangzhou in 1279. The invaders, who already controlled the north of the country, thus unified the entire territory under a new dynasty of foreign origin called the Yuan Dynasty. The founder of the Yuan Dynasty was Kublai Khan, who was ruling the country when Marco Polo arrived in China from Venice.

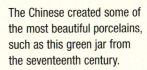

The Chinese created some of the most beautiful porcelains, such as this green jar from the seventeenth century.

## FROM THE MING DYNASTY TO TODAY

The Chinese people, subject to the rule of a foreign dynasty, were stirred toward revolt by intense fiscal pressure and by natural disasters that caused periods of severe famine. Under these circumstances, a Buddhist monk of humble peasant origins led the opposition against the foreign dynasty. After defeating the Yuan, he was proclaimed the first emperor of the new Ming Dynasty (1368–1644) under the name of Hongwu. His grandson, Yongle, (1402–1424) moved the capital city from Nanjing to Peking. From that period on, Chinese emperors lived in isolation behind the walls of the Forbidden City, which they left only once a year to participate in a ceremony of prayer to their ancestors.

Contacts with the outside world multiplied during the Ming Dynasty. In the fourteenth century, the famous navigator Zheng He traversed the archipelagos of Southeast Asia, India, Persia, and even Africa and Australia. Not much later, the first Portuguese navigators made their appearance on the Chinese coasts. The presence of missionaries and Western traders soon became an everyday sight in coastal cities. In 1644, a popular uprising against the growing despotism of the emperors favored the overthrow of the Ming Dynasty by the Manchus, who invaded the country from the north. Without delay, the Manchus founded a new dynasty, the Qing ("pure") Dynasty (1644–1911). The most important members of this lineage were the Kangxi (1662–1722), the Yongzheng (1723–1735), and the Qianlong (1736–1795).

The Qing Dynasty was the last imperial line to govern China. It was overthrown in 1911. The country suffered through a series of revolutions until, in 1949, Mao Tse-tung proclaimed the People's Republic of China, establishing a totalitarian Communist regime that has lasted to the present day.

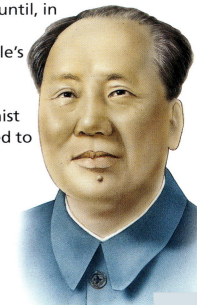

The Chinese dynasty tradition of thirty-four hundred years collapsed at the beginning of the twentieth century. In 1949, Mao Tse-tung (or Mao Zedong, 1893–1976), after a long civil war, proclaimed the People's Republic of China.

# THE FIRST EMPEROR OF CHINA

In the year 259 B.C., a wealthy Chinese merchant had a son named Cheng. This merchant managed to occupy the throne of the Qin kingdom in 250 B.C., and passed it on as an inheritance to his son, Cheng, in 246 B.C. Military victory over the neighboring states in 221 B.C. inspired Cheng to change his name to Qin Shi Huangdi, which means the first (*shi*) revered emperor (*huangdi*) of China (*Qin*).

**death**
Qin Shi Huangdi died in 210 B.C., far from his land, while he was seeking the elixir of immortality

**mausoleum**
long before he died, he had an enormous mausoleum built at the foot of Mount Li

**hill**
the burial of the emperor and his funeral trousseau are placed underneath an artificial hill, on which trees and plants were planted

**terracotta army** ■
a terracotta reproduction of the imperial army extends around the burial site

**in combat** ■
the terracotta army occupies four ditches surrounded by the earth walls, and is arranged in a similar way to actual combat formations

**cavalry** ■
cavalry soldiers drawing the bridles of their mounts are represented in the third level

**Chinese writing system**

Among the principal achievements of Qin Shi Huangdi are the construction of a great communications network and the standardization of weights, measures, and the Chinese writing system. For example, a pictogram drawing that resembles a mother with a baby carries an implicit idea, in this case the concept of "mother." There are also phonograms, or characters that indicate the sound of each image.

## CHINA COMES FROM QIN

The Qin Dynasty, founded by the first emperor, disappeared shortly after his death, but left an imposing legacy that includes the Great Wall, a monumental burial style, a standardized writing system, and the name by which the country is known today; the term *China* comes from "Qin."

**■ archers**
soldiers equipped with ballistas (catapults that fired spears) and archers were arranged in a way that enabled them to protect their comrades

**■ servants and workers**
many servants of the court and workers who had participated in the building of the imperial tomb were also buried in the mausoleum

**5,000 figures ■**
terracotta army contains a total of 5,000 figures, each with a face having individualized features

**infantry ■**
light infantry soldiers, who wear very little protective armor, are in the first rows

**breastplates ■**
soldiers protected with breastplates and equipped with iron lances are found in the second section

# A DEFENSE AGAINST INVASIONS

The late period of the Zhou Dynasty is known as the Era of the Warring Kingdoms, because the territory was divided into various kingdoms that constantly fought each other and their northern neighbors, the Hiung-nu. These nomadic people tried to invade China to pillage the country and take control of its wealth. In order to defend themselves against these fearsome warriors, the kingdoms of Qin, Zhao, and Yan each constructed their own wall. After the unification of China by the first emperor, he ordered the joining of these three fragments to create the Great Wall.

### ■ chronology
the Great Wall was built around the year 221 B.C., and was extended and rebuilt on various later occasions under the Ming Dynasty period (1368–1644)

### ■ World Heritage Site
this wall is the most brilliant and gigantic works of military engineering; as a result, it has been declared a World Heritage Site

### ■ name
in Chinese historical records, it was named "the great wall ten thousand li in length," meaning "the three thousand-mile long great wall"

### ■ dimensions
the Great Wall is actually more than thirty-one hundred miles long, between twenty-two and twenty-six feet high on average, and the encircling battlements are eighteen feet wide

**The Manchu invasion**

Despite its size and the effort it took to build it, the Great Wall was not able to impede invasions, which occurred repeatedly through China's history. In 1644, the Manchus crossed over it by scaling the walls, and with the assistance of a Chinese traitor who left a gate open.

### ■ reinforcements
throughout its length, the Great Wall is reinforced by a tower every 1.5 miles, a guard post every 3 miles, a fort every 9 miles, and a barracks every 31 miles

### FROM THE MOON
Astronauts say that the Great Wall is the only structure built by humankind that can be seen from the moon. Viewed from space, its zigzagging course underlines the importance of a great work that has survived into our time in a condition very similar to what it was after the last rebuilding.

### ■ materials
packed earth, reinforced with stones, and in some stretches covered with ceramic, was used in its construction

### ■ workers
work was carried out by some three hundred thousand forced laborers, including slaves, prisoners of war, and convicts, who often died during the project

### ■ extension
it stretches westward, through an area of undulating mountains, from the Jiayu Pass, in the province of Gansu, to the mouth of the Yalu River, in the province of Liaoning

### ■ couriers
imperial couriers were able to use the Great Wall's buildings to sleep or rest

### ■ lookouts
guards stationed on the towers were able to spot an enemy at a great distance, and to send signals from one tower to the next to request information

# BUDDHISM, THE SEARCH FOR PARADISE

The three major religions of China are Confucianism, Taoism, and Buddhism. The first two arose within China itself, while Buddhism arrived from India. All three religions share the basic concepts of achieving the harmony of humanity with the universe, and of following the path that leads each human being to wisdom. Since the beginning of the fourth century, Buddhism has been China's dominant religion, thanks to the protection it was granted by the emperors.

■ **Siddhartha Gautama**
creator of Buddhism was born around the year 560 B.C. as Siddhartha Gautama

■ **prince**
he was the son of a king, and his father forbade him from leaving the palace to prevent him from knowing the harsh reality of life

■ **the four encounters**
one day, the young man left the palace, disobeying his father, and had four encounters that changed his life

**CONFUCIUS**

Confucius (551–479 B.C.) was the creator of Confucianism, known in China as the "school of the learned." This wise man proposed that people should struggle to reach a better state through self-knowledge, a desire for heaven, and the practice of virtues such as devotion, loyalty, benevolence, justice, and self-discipline.

■ **3. the dead man**
he subsequently encountered a funeral possession carrying human remains

**1. the old man** ■
his first encounter was with an old man, doubled over, who stumbled as he walked, supported by his cane

**2. the sick man** ■
his second encounter was with a person who suffered the pains of a terrible illness

Lao-tsu created Taoism and synthesized it in his work *Tao te king*. In this book he suggested a return to nature, a search for immortality, and abandoning politics to concentrate on the essence of human nature. Taoism was the religion of the people.

**The Taoism of Lao-tsu**

■ **4. the saint**

when he was on his way back to the palace, he encountered a saint whose face radiated peace and happiness

■ **the truth**

as a result of these four encounters, the young man decided to renounce his comfortable palace life, and dedicate the rest of his life to the search for truth

■ **illumination**

that same night, he secretly abandoned his father's palace, and began a spiritual search that helped him to reach illumination, known as *nirvana* in Buddhist terms

■ **Buddha**

after that, he was called Buddha, which means "that which is totally conscious," or Shakyamuni, "the sage of the shakyas"

12
13

# A FANTASTIC PYRAMID OF TILES

The pagoda originated in India as a monument to guard the relics of Buddha. It came to China through Central Asia, together with the Buddhist religion, and was transformed to conform with the Chinese architectural tradition of towered pavilions. Indeed, it was in China that the pagoda was given its characteristic form, and it was then exported to other countries, such as Japan. The oldest Chinese pagoda known today dates back to the year 532.

## ARCHITECTURE IN WOOD

In China, the most valued construction material was always wood. For this reason, only buildings of limited height and technical complexity could be constructed. Most Chinese buildings are characterized by horizontal development, with the pagoda being the only notable exception.

The stupa, a predecessor of the pagoda, was created by the Hindu emperor Ashoka to preserve and adore Buddha's relics. It is a round building topped by a vertical axis with umbrellas, and equipped with encircling galleries so that worshippers can walk around the monument. It has four doors facing toward the four cardinal compass points.

**The Hindu stupa**

■ **materials** ■
the oldest pagodas were made of wood, and because of this, have not survived into the present; later pagodas were made of brick and stone

■ **pagoda of Shakyamuni**
one of the most complex pagodas known, Shakyamuni, in Ying Xian, has five stories and is octagonal in shape

**tiled roof** ■

their most outstanding feature is their superimposed varnished tiles, the size of which diminish progressively, to make the roofs

■ **location**

pagodas could be part of temples or monasteries, but were also built on hills and mountains so that they could play protective or magical roles

**layout** ■

the majority of pagodas are laid out in a square or polygonal form, and reach great heights

■ **worship**

worshippers were not allowed inside the sacred pagoda, but had to stand around the building in order to worship or invoke their gods

**statues** ■

in classical pagodas, the lower floors house chapels with religious statues, and the upper floor serves to accentuate the dignity of the building

■ **Buddhas**

on the lower floor of the pagoda of Shakyamuni, there is an enthroned Buddha, thirty-six feet high, and statues of the four mystic Buddhas are found on the upper floors

# THE LABOR-INTENSIVE CULTIVATION OF RICE

For thousands of years in Chinese history, agriculture has been the basis of the economy and the foundation for the life of the state. Agriculture produced the food necessary to prevent starvation, and was the source of rich tributes that added to the wealth of the state. Nevertheless, most of the peasants were poor, and their work-filled lives knew no other joys than the seasonal festivals. The most important crop was rice, which today is still the staple food of the Chinese people.

**families** ■
agricultural cultivation was done by families, who distributed the various tasks to be performed among their members

**method of cultivation** ■
in order for rice to grow more rapidly, with less waste of water, and a more abundant harvest, they began to plant rice instead of sowing it

**houses**
peasant families lived in simple houses made of mud, wood, and vegetable fibers, located near the fields they cultivated

**peasants** ■
peasants made up the lowest social class inside the Chinese state, and could neither read nor write

**germination**
the process began by placing the seeds in baskets, which were then placed into water to promote germination

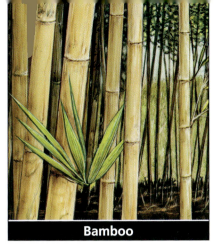

**Bamboo**

In the woods of China, several plants, such as bamboo, grow, and the inhabitants of the country have utilized it well. The Chinese have used bamboo to make furniture and many other objects for everyday use, such as walking sticks, umbrellas, or baskets.

## TEA

Tea is a plant originally from China; it did not arrive in Europe until the sixteenth century. According to legend, the first tea leaves emerged when a Buddhist monk cut out his eyelids to stop him from closing his eyes, enabling him to dedicate himself to meditation. Tea drinking became widespread in China during the Tang Dynasty.

### ■ irrigation
a mechanism operated manually allowed adjustment of the water level in the fields

### ■ planting
after they germinated, the sprouts were planted in a field and surrounded with dikes

### ■ dikes
fields were nearly always laid out in marshy areas, on the shores of rivers or lakes, and were protected from periodic floods with the use of dikes

### harvest
when the rice had already grown and ripened, the plants were cut with sickles and transported to the threshing area

### threshing
in the threshing area, the plants were spread over the ground for threshing, or separation of the grain from the straw

# URBAN LIFE DURING THE SONG ERA

The first Chinese cities emerged in ancient eras, even before the reign of the first emperor. In the beginning, cities primarily fulfilled administrative functions, as the majority of their inhabitants were officials of the state. With the passage of time, the cities lost their administrative importance, and came to be, above all, centers for commerce, handicraft, and communication. The appearance of the cities also changed, because the walls were limited to city centers or disappeared entirely.

**commercial stalls ■**
selling posts offered their customers foods, items of clothing, and products for everyday use made by craftsmen

**■ canals**
most cities were located on the banks of rivers or canals, as these were the primary avenues of transportation

**■ merchandise**
most merchandise arrived in the city through waterways, in boats specially designed to navigate rivers and canals

**■ porters**
porters carried on their right shoulder a rod that held a basket full of products on each end

## ADMINISTRATORS

In China, administrative officials filled a role similar to that of the aristocracy in Europe. They wore special clothes that varied according to their rank, so that one could recognize each type of official by his attire.

## CHINA'S RIVERS

The main rivers of China are the Huang-He, the Yang-tse Kiang, and the Xi Jiang. All three flow from the western highlands toward the Pacific Ocean, flood periodically, and are connected by an important network of canals.

■ **transportation**
products were moved from one place to another on the backs of animals or on the shoulders of porters

■ **wheelbarrow**
another means of transport was the wheelbarrow, a Chinese invention equipped with an enormous wheel; sometimes, it was helped by a sail

**platforms** ■
persons of high rank were moved in portable platforms carried by two or more porters

■ **buildings**
nearly all the buildings in the cities were made of wood and had only one story

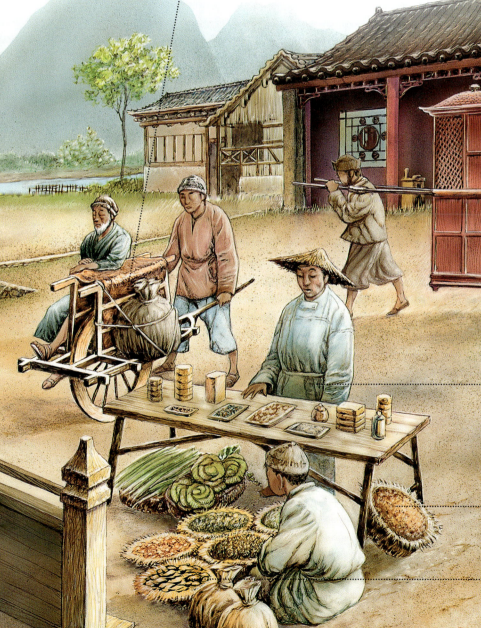

■ **dynamism**
the cities were full of life; merchandise was loaded and unloaded items were bought and sold; products were moved from one place to the other; and food was offered for sale outdoors

■ **vegetable fibers**
parasols, portable platforms, and baskets were made of vegetable fibers

■ **commerce**
commerce took place along the commercial streets, where the vendors would set up their movable sales posts

# A LUXURY PRODUCT COVETED IN THE WEST

The process of obtaining silk has been documented in China since Neolithic times, that is to say, some seven thousand years before our time. For a long time, silk was a product made exclusively in China, and was highly coveted among the most powerful classes in Europe. This fact is at the basis of the so-called Silk Route, a commercial pathway across which caravans transported silk and other products from China to the West.

**cocoons** ■
at a certain point, silkworms form cocoons, and remain inside for two weeks before passing into the next phase

**women** ■
in ancient China, silk production was a job done exclusively by women

## PORCELAIN

After the sixth century, silk ceased to be the primary export from China. From that time on, the Silk Route brought other products coveted in Europe, especially spices and porcelain, which was made exclusively in China.

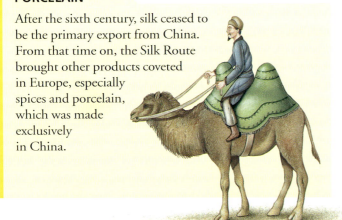

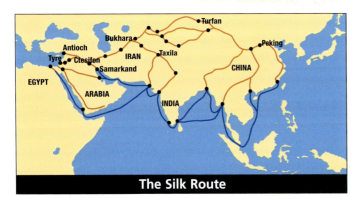

**The Silk Route**

The Silk Route, which grew out of commercial interests, ended up becoming a route for the circulation of ideas, culture, and art between East and West. Buddhism arrived in China by means of the Silk Route, and several travelers who traversed either the entire route or part of it, wrote about their impressions in travel accounts.

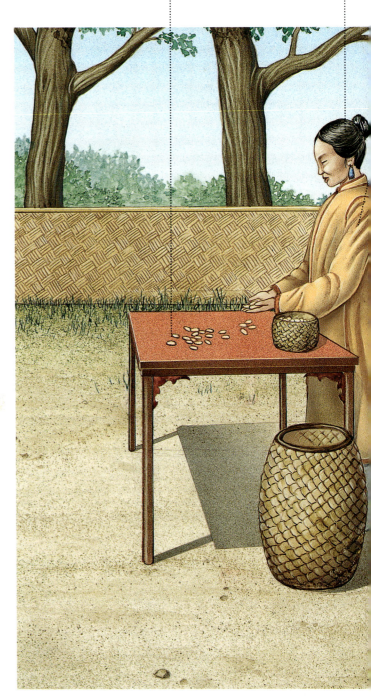

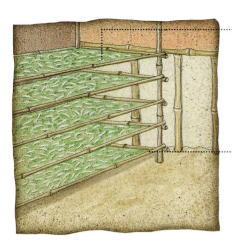

### ■ worms
the first step consisted of raising silkworms, who were fed with freshly-picked white mulberries

### ■ trays
silkworms were kept in trays that were heated to promote development

### ■ mulberry tree
this tree-like plant that grows up to twenty feet tall, has been cultivated since very ancient times in China. It was introduced in Europe in the mid-fifteenth century

### ■ uses
in addition to making garments, silk was also used to upholster furniture and walls, or as a base for writing and painting

### silk
silk production is a long and difficult process that begins with the process of "drowning the cocoon" using water vapor

### fibers
while submerging the cocoons in water heated to 194°, the process of winding the silk threads begins; then they are left to dry in the sun

### raw silk
silk obtained in this manner is called raw or unprocessed silk, and can be dyed different colors with natural dyes

### fabrics
subsequently, the threads are prepared in different ways for their insertion into the loom, where silk fabrics come out

# AN ITALIAN IN THE GREAT KHAN'S COURT

The Venetian Marco Polo was just seventeen years old in 1271, when he left for China with his father, Niccolò, and his uncle, Matteo, who were merchants. The young man arrived in China in 1275, at a time when Kublai Khan governed the country. Polo was the first European to visit China, and thanks to his descriptions of this country, Europeans got to know about its rivers, its cities, and the life of its people. Until that time, to Westerners, China was synonymous with terror.

## CHINA AND THE WEST

For a long time, China and the West were two worlds isolated from each other, and practically unknown to each other. The accounts of travelers were the first news to reach Europe regarding the nature, customs, and the economy of the world in the East.

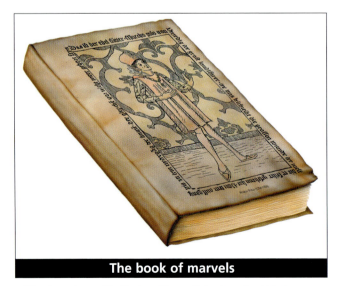

### The book of marvels

After he returned to Venice, Marco Polo described his journey in a book that has become known as *The Book of Marvels.* His highly favorable descriptions gave rise in the West to the notion that the East was a place of fabulous wealth; this later helped facilitate the great age of geographical discoveries.

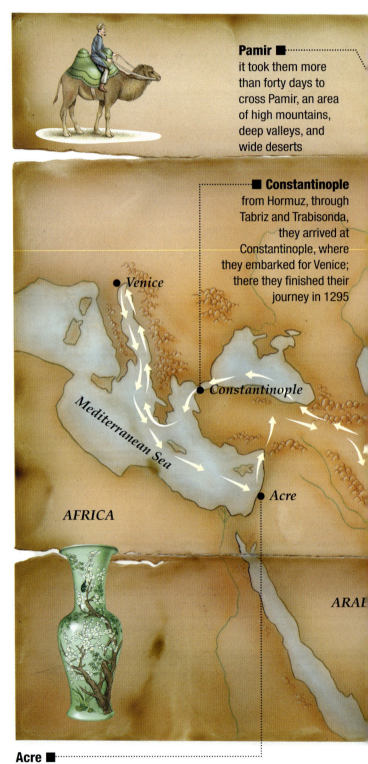

**Pamir ■**
it took them more than forty days to cross Pamir, an area of high mountains, deep valleys, and wide deserts

**■ Constantinople**
from Hormuz, through Tabriz and Trabisonda, they arrived at Constantinople, where they embarked for Venice; there they finished their journey in 1295

Venice

*Mediterranean Sea*

*Constantinople*

*Acre*

AFRICA

ARAB

**Acre ■**
the Polos first went to Acre, the city of the Crusades, and from there passed through Armenia on the way to the Persian Gulf

**The Lob Desert** ■
About the Lob (Gobi) Desert, Marco Polo said that he would need more than a year to cross it, and that there were only twenty-eight oases in the entire desert

**Camcio** ■
in Camcio (Kan-cheu), a place that, in the words of Marco Polo, was "not worth mentioning," the travelers stayed a year for business reasons

**Shang-tu** ■
The Polo party passed through Erzina and Karakorum before arriving at Shang-tu, where the Great Khan had his summer home

**■ Cambaluc**
Cambaluc, today Beijing, did not impress Marco Polo as much as Hang-cheu, about which he said, "it is the greatest city on earth."

**Su-cheu** ■
the first Chinese city reached by Marco Polo and the others was Su-cheu. There, they were most impressed by its temples and Buddhist monasteries

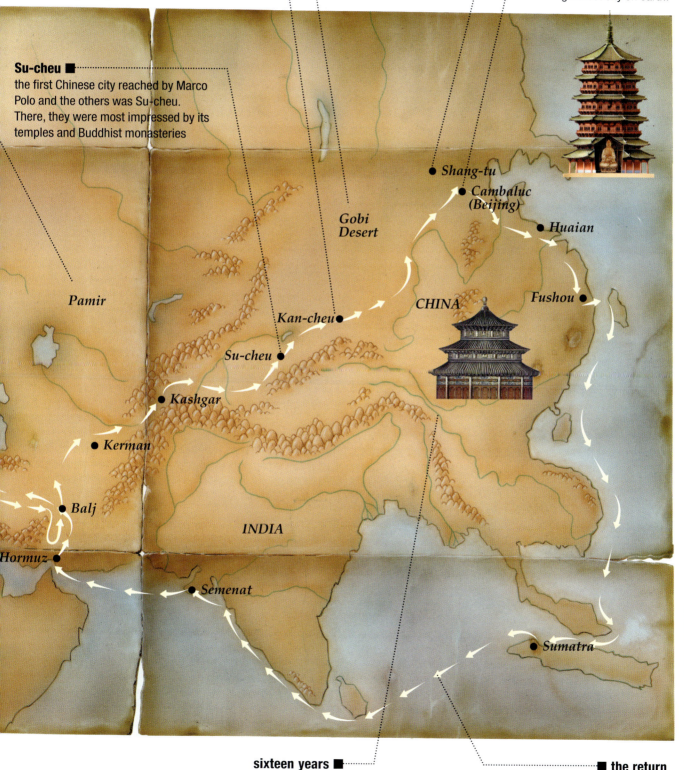

**sixteen years** ■
during the sixteen years that he stayed in China, Marco Polo traveled across the country and the neighboring areas as a diplomatic envoy of the Great Khan

**■ the return**
the Polo party returned to Europe by sea, in a voyage that lasted three years and carried them to Hormuz

# CHINA'S GREATEST CONTRIBUTIONS

The development of science and technology in China goes back several thousand years before Christ, when inventions such as the manual spindle, the technique for founding iron, and the first calendar were established. Subsequently, inventions were produced almost without interruption. China brought to the world such important products as paper, ink, a staff for holding spun fabrics, the compass, and gunpowder. The Chinese also invented a printing system that was unknown in Europe when Gutenberg created his moveable type press.

**1. bamboo**
in the beginning, paper was produced from bamboo rods that had to be soaked for more than one hundred days

**2. mixing**
later, the rods were peeled, ground, and mixed with a lime solution to form a dough that was boiled for eight days

**3. paper paste** ■
the fibrous paste that was formed was mixed with water and a chemical solution inside a barrel

**4. sheets of paper** ■
thin layers of paste that formed sheets of paper were removed from the water with a sieve

### paper

is one of the most important inventions in the history of civilization; it was made for the first time in China during the Han Dynasty

### Cai Lun

Chinese historical records show that Cai Lun, an official in the imperial workshops, invented paper in the year 105

### writing media

before the invention of paper, silk strips, bones, turtle shells, stones, strips of bamboo, or wooden tablets were used to hold written works

### ink

ink and the brushes were also invented during the Han Dynasty, greatly enhancing the spread of writing

**Zhang Heng's seismograph**

Between the first and second centuries, Chinese scientist Zhang Heng invented an early seismograph, an instrument for detecting earthquakes. When the first tremors were produced, the device activated a ball that fell into the mouth of a frog through the mouth of a dragon; according to the position of the frog, one could tell where the earthquake took place.

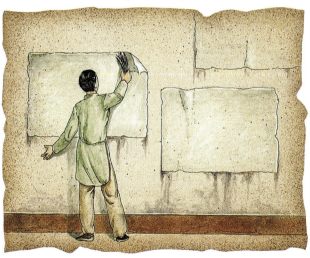

### 5. drying

the process of producing paper was finished when the sheets were brushed against a hot wall to dry them

## GUNPOWDER

In the ninth century, Chinese alchemists who were trying to obtain the elixir of immortality, discovered gunpowder. The search for this elixir led them to prove that an explosion was produced when mixing sulfur, saltpeter, and vegetable carbon, and then applying a spark to the mixture. There is evidence that projectiles of gunpowder, were already in use in the year 904. This invention arrived in Europe in the twelfth century.

# FROM ONE PLACE TO ANOTHER

The wheel had been in China since ancient times, and carts and wheelbarrows were known means of transportation. However, people usually moved and transported loads on foot or on the backs of horses or camels. The emperor and some privileged citizens could travel in carts, carriages, or on portable platforms. Ground transportation was difficult because of the long distances and because many roads were impassable during certain seasons of the year. Therefore, the preferred means of transportation were rivers and canals, which were always lined with small boats.

**portable platforms ■**
the imperial platforms were much larger and more luxurious than those of any other citizen

**cortege ■**
behind the emperor, his family members or officials traveled on luxuriously decorated platforms

**weapons ■**
in the mounted guard, there were men armed with lances, axes, darts, and arrows; there were also standard bearers

**servants ■**
the cortege also included servants, who carried useful objects such as umbrellas or fans

**ladder ■**
the small ladder, carried by two servants, was used to climb on and off a carriage or platform

**uniforms ■**
the men of the mounted guard wore different uniforms depending on the weapons they carried

**■ luxury**
the splendor and luxury of the court accompanied the emperor even when he was moving from place to place

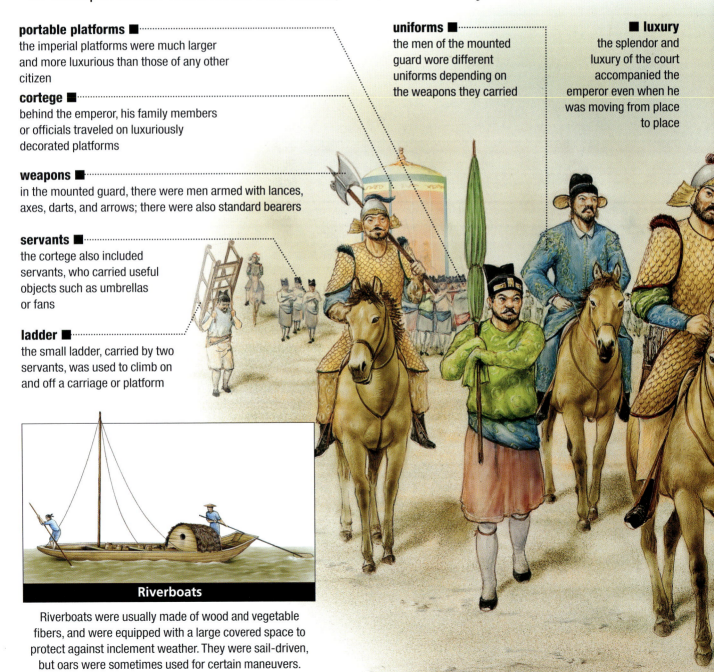

**Riverboats**

Riverboats were usually made of wood and vegetable fibers, and were equipped with a large covered space to protect against inclement weather. They were sail-driven, but oars were sometimes used for certain maneuvers.

## THE MAIL

The imperial mail service was created by the first emperor, Qin Shi Huangdi. Couriers, mounted on horseback, transmitted messages from the emperor or high-ranking dignitaries, and carried administrative documents. All over the country, there were places where they could rest and sleep.

**carriage** ■
unlike the common people, the emperor traveled in a luxury carriage drawn by horses

■ **mounted guard**
security was the responsibility of mounted guards, who were armed and prepared to confront any enemy

# A SECRET DWELLING FOR THE EMPEROR

The emperor was the highest authority in China and the most important figure in the country. He was obliged to govern his people, to exert himself to maintain the peace, to proclaim the calendar each year, and to carry out various rituals to assure the fertility of the harvests. From the time of the Ming Dynasty, Chinese emperors lived in seclusion in the great imperial palace in Peking, known as the Forbidden City.

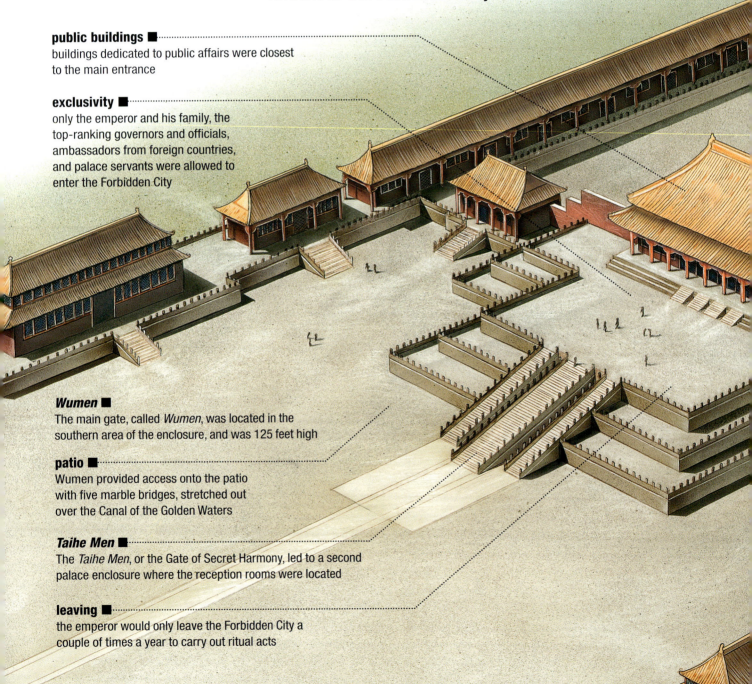

**public buildings** ■
buildings dedicated to public affairs were closest to the main entrance

**exclusivity** ■
only the emperor and his family, the top-ranking governors and officials, ambassadors from foreign countries, and palace servants were allowed to enter the Forbidden City

**Wumen** ■
The main gate, called *Wumen*, was located in the southern area of the enclosure, and was 125 feet high

**patio** ■
Wumen provided access onto the patio with five marble bridges, stretched out over the Canal of the Golden Waters

**Taihe Men** ■
The *Taihe Men*, or the Gate of Secret Harmony, led to a second palace enclosure where the reception rooms were located

**leaving** ■
the emperor would only leave the Forbidden City a couple of times a year to carry out ritual acts

**■ walls**
the Forbidden City is a rectangular enclosure, completely surrounded by walls

**■ area**
the Forbidden City occupies an area of 178 acres, and more than two hundred thousand workers helped to build it

**private buildings ■**
the private quarters for the emperor and his family were located at the back of the enclosure, in the northern section

**The Temple of Heaven**

The day before the winter solstice, the emperor, accompanied by a procession, walked from the Forbidden City to the Temple of Heaven, to the south of the city. There, at the Altar of Heaven, he presented his report about the events that occurred during the year and made the appropriate sacrifices.

## EUNUCHS

Eunuchs were impotent men. Evidence of eunuchs appears in most kingdoms in the ancient world, but in no other country were they as important as in China. They served in the imperial palace to bring up children, to guard the harem, and to act as spies.

# GREAT PERIODS IN CHINA'S HISTORY

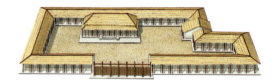

| | |
|---|---|
| Neolithic period | 7000–1500 B.C. |
| Shang Dynasty | 1500–1050 B.C. |
| Zhou Dynasty | 1050–221 B.C. |
| Qin Empire | 221 B.C.–206 B.C. |
| Han Dynasty | 206 B.C.–220 A.D. |
| The Three Kingdoms | 225–265 |
| The Six Dynasties | 265–429 |
| Tang Dynasty | 618–907 |
| The Five Kingdoms and the Ten States | 907–1002 |
| Northern Song Dynasty | 1002–1127 |
| Southern Song Dynasty | 1127–1279 |
| Yuan Dynasty | 1279–1368 |
| Ming Dynasty | 1368–1644 |
| Qing (Manchu) Dynasty | 1644–1911 |
| Opium War | 1839–1842 |
| People's Republic of China | 1949 |

# TO LEARN MORE
## DID YOU KNOW...?

… some seven thousand years before modern times, the Chinese made stone implements for defense and hunting, and ceramic containers for the preparation and preservation of food?

… important archeological remains are preserved at Anyang, one of the last capitals of the Shang Dynasty?

… in the oldest cities of China, only people of high rank could live in the city center, while artisans and merchants, for example, had to live in areas located outside the city walls?

… Kublai Khan was the grandson of Genghis Khan, the Mongol chief who unified the nomadic tribes of his people and founded a great empire that extended from China to the Urals?

… the first missionary who preached Christianity in China was the Spanish Jesuit priest Francisco Xavier, who died in that country in 1552?

… Jesuit, Franciscan, and Dominican missionaries were the main sources for the spread of Western culture and customs in China?

… the emperor Kangxi (1662–1722) divided Peking into two sectors so that the Manchus would not intermingle with the Chinese, and required the Chinese to wear their hair in a braid as a sign of submission?

… all the European royal palaces of the eighteenth century had at least one Chinese room, where the walls were covered with porcelain plaques or silks from that faraway country?

… China waged the Opium War (1839–1842) against Great Britain; the war ended with the signing of the Treaty of Nanjing; Chinese ceded Hong Kong to the British, and opened several cities to Western trade?

# CHINA TODAY

| | |
|---|---|
| **Total area** | 2,365,500 square acres |
| **Population** | 1.3 billion |
| **Population Density** | 351 people per square mile |
| **Capital** | Beijing (formerly known as "Peking") |
| **Official currency** | the yuan |
| **Distance N-S** | 3,666 miles |
| **Distance E-W** | 3,106 miles |
| **Main rivers** | Yang-tse Kiang (3,718 miles long) Huang He or Yellow River (3,012 miles long) |
| **Types of Vegetables** | More than thirty thousand |

# INDEX